THE EGG TIMER

LIBREX

01704

1704

For Emma
and Mark Percival

William Heinemann Ltd
Michelin House, 81 Fulham Road
London SW3 6RB

LONDON   MELBOURNE   AUCKLAND

First published 1993
Reprinted 1995
Text © 1993 William Mayne
Illustrations © 1993 Anthony Lewis
The right of William Mayne to be
identified as author of this work has been
asserted by him in accordance with the
Copyrights, Designs and Patents Act 1988
ISBN 0 434 97676 8
Produced by Mandarin Offset
Printed in China

A school pack of SUPERCHAMPS 19–24
is available from
Heinemann Educational Books
ISBN 0 435 00093 4

Chapter 1

THE SKIBATHY FAMILY was at Tullamarine airport, Melbourne, very early. People were arriving at Arrivals, but everybody had departed from Departures and everything was closed.

'We're here too soon, Wainwright,' said Mum. 'I haven't slept, I know, and I'm cold.'

Dad's name was Wainwright, like a family name. He was actually George first, as well. 'Bound to be a nip in the air.' Then he looked at the clock. 'Quarter to six?' he said. 'That's ridiculously early. That's even before the alarm should have rung to wake us. And look, the date is the thirty-third of August. I hope they run their schedules better.'

Melinda did some mental arithmetic about the date, but Wayne got there first. 'September the second,' he said. 'You'll learn it next year in Fourth Grade.' Wayne was a modern form of Wainwright. He was George second.

'Are we at Inland yet?' asked Dora. 'There isn't nobody here.' She shook her doll Toota, in case it was naughty.

'England,' said Melinda, about as nicely as she could at that time of day.

'We'll soon be on the aeroplane,' said

Mum, picking Dora up.

'It would be sooner if we'd got here later,' said Melinda. Wayne began to argue with her about it. Mum stopped strife by sending them to ride the escalators, which no one was using.

'I can't understand leaving so early,' said Dad. 'You'll see when we get back. The alarm was set for six, to get straight up and into the car and drive from Ivanhoe, be here for seven and check in.'

'We're here,' said Mum. 'That's what counts.'

But Dad shook his head. 'Not like me to get a detail like that wrong,' he muttered (and Mum smiled, because she knew Dad). 'Hey, look, they're opening up the coffee bar.'

When they were in aeroplane time no one could tell when it was or where they were. The day went on for ever, and Dad became quiet, Wayne's head ached, Melinda felt sick, Dora would not speak, and only Mum could smile now and then. At last they got out at London. It was the thirty-fourth or thirty-fifth of August.

'I must be jet-lagged,' said Mum, in the hotel. 'I've ordered tea for six, because I keep thinking that's how many we are.'

'It's because it's Inland,' said Dora, thinking about it.

The next day the train broke down, on the way to look at the Vikings. It stopped at a station and could not get started again. English people in the next seats said it was typical, except about being conveniently at a station.

'I was once three weeks getting to Alice Springs,' said Dad. 'Going so slow I saw the grass grow, no station for ten days.'

Melinda watched a pigeon. Wayne saw a clock getting older. The guard made them all get off because of a mechanical fault. People made a fuss, but Dad said,

'It'll be right. You stay here, Mum, and the girls. Wayne and I will get the info.'

Everybody else from the train was wanting the same things too, and there was a queue. Dad was never able to stand in line for an information counter. 'Watching the grass grow,' he said. 'No way. Once in a lifetime is enough for me. I'll take a look round, and you keep a place in the traffic for me.' And off he went.

Wayne found himself alone, if you didn't count all the strangers, the other side of the world from home. He yawned. He searched his pocket for a lolly. He shuffled his feet. He stood there. He yawned again and his eyes went misty.

Then he was not alone. There was a boy standing beside him, and they were talking. At least, the boy was. 'You want to come and look at this,' he said. 'You'll like this. You will.' That was what he meant, but Wayne had to fill in the words.

Instead of keeping his place in the queue he was going out of the station, unable to decide whether he was alone or with the boy.

'Look,' said the boy, by waving his hand. Wayne saw his own name, Skibathy, written in large white letters on a black background. The letters wavered.

Dad was jogging his arm. 'You're asleep like a horse,' he said, 'on all four feet. But if you fall over you won't get crushed in the stampede.' Because no one was moving. 'Who was your friend? You don't know anyone here.'

'I was dreaming,' said Wayne. 'Wait here, Dad. I've got to go somewhere a minute.'

'Toilets over there,' said Dad. But Wayne was looking for something else outside in the street. Before he could bring Dad to it, it had gone. He watched it out of sight.

'I'm still dreaming,' he thought. 'Must be.' He went back to Dad and said nothing because it must be a mistake.

Dad was at the counter, finding out all sorts of stuff and stowing pieces of paper in his pockets.

'That's it,' he said. 'On our way in no time, half an hour or so. They're very nice about it, considering it's their fault.'

'I expect I'm jet-lagged,' said Wayne. 'But outside the station there was a bus going to places written on the front.'

'Yeah,' said Dad. 'Tram says Coburg, it's where it goes, eh?'

'One of the names,' said Wayne, 'was Skibathy. It was going to a place called Skibathy.'

'You sure, Wayne?' said Dad, dropping the rest of the papers. 'Show me.'

'It's gone there,' said Wayne. 'It went up the road.'

'Go and get the girls,' said Dad. 'We'll look into this.'

Chapter 2

ONE THING ABOUT Dad, he knew when to believe you, and he knew what to do about it. He had done it when Wayne came back with the others. He had gone out into the street, got the truth from a taxi driver, and had the door open ready.

'All fixed up,' he said. 'We're staying at the pub, the Lord Something Arms. The last bus this week just went so we've got the taxi. This is really going to be interesting.'

'But Toota is in London,' said Dora.

'All alone.'

'We'll call the hotel,' said Mum. 'Well, we'd better all get in and find what's what, shall we, Wainwright?' She was used to Dad doing sudden things. It was what she first liked about him.

'Right on,' said Dad. 'Take her away, mate.'

'It's just a little village,' said the driver. 'Nothing ever happened there. There's nothing famous.'

Dad explained how Australians like to know where they came from and how far they went back. 'We'll be descended from the squire,' he said. 'That's how it goes. That's famous to me. It'll be a long way back in time.' He was right.

The driver was right. Skibathy was the pub, a tiny shop, and a few cottages. 'Nice,' said Mum. 'Quaint.'

Dad paid the taxi.

'Six of you,' said the man.

'Five,' said Dad. 'Three kids, the wife, and I.'

'Thought it was six,' said the driver. 'You sure?'

'He would mean Toota,' said Dora, 'if Toota would have been here.'

At the pub, Dad was sure everyone would be related to him, but the landlady said only the village had the name Skibathy, and how long were they staying?

'Everybody here is called Wainwright,' she said. 'My husband was Walter, the shop is George and missus, and next there's the two old ladies, Ethel and Marigold.' She went through them all.

'It's the right place,' said Dad. 'My name's Wainwright, too. We must have come from here.'

'You could ask the vicar,' said Mrs

Wainwright. 'We share him with the
next village and he lives there. Even Lord
Granger's house fell into ruin a hundred
years ago. Now, there's a room for you
two, another for the little girls, and one
for the two boys.'

'Just one boy,' said Mum. 'I get that
feeling sometimes, too.'

'They're as like as two eggs,' said Mrs
Wainwright.

Dad went out again and took photographs of everyone called Wainwright, whether they liked it or not. Dad liked, so that was that. He liked instant pictures too, without wanting to wait three minutes for them. He stowed them in his pocket as they came from the camera and forgot them until he was eating soup that evening.

'You're all splashing like brumbies at a

water-hole,' he said. 'Just watch it, eh? There's gravy on these old ladies, Ethel and Marigold.'

'No it isn't,' said Melinda. 'It's Wayne. I knew he looked funny, but not like a tin of Campbell's.'

'He was here all the time,' said Mum. 'It can't be Wayne.'

It wasn't soup. It wasn't Wayne. But there was someone in the picture of Ethel and Marigold who hadn't been there when it was taken.

There was someone extra, too, in the photo of George and missus, and a spare figure standing beside the Wainwrights from the end cottage. It was never very clear, but it was always the same person, rather like Wayne, but not him.

'It's the flash,' said Dad. 'They've got it wrong. I'll get a new film from the makers.'

'If it had have been Wayne you'd need a new camera,' said Melinda. 'And his ring-in isn't much better.'

'Shut up,' said Dad. 'This is serious. The camera's picked up the family ghost, that's what.'

'Careful what you say,' said Mum. 'We haven't got Toota to help us go to sleep.'

'There's one left in the pack,' said Dad. 'Mrs Wainwright, please take a picture of us all while we eat our cutlets. Then we'll see who's extra.'

Mrs Wainwright looked at the picture. 'That's him,' she said. 'I thought there were six of you, and there he is.'

'Is it a g, o, a, s, t?' asked Mum, shaky on her spelling.

'That'll be it,' said Mrs Wainwright. 'He'll have been somebody, but I don't know who. He's a Wainwright too, judging by the ears with their pointy tops.

I'll tell you what, Mr Skibathy, you brought that with you. It's no one we know.'

They forgot about ghosts when Wayne remembered that it was Saturday, the night he usually went to the Bowlorama.

'It was last night at home this morning,' said Dad. 'Now it's Sunday.'

Melinda shook her head. She knew it couldn't be true, and that days happened at the same time everywhere, otherwise nothing made sense.

Chapter 3

THE NEXT DAY WAS Sunday in Skibathy, whatever it was anywhere else. 'We'll go to church,' said Dad.

Melinda expected something like a wedding with smart people and cake afterwards. Wayne thought of a cathedral. Dora thought about Toota. Mum was worried about not having a hat. Dad said that what was good enough for God's outback was good enough for his parlour, and went in a Surfers' Paradise T-shirt.

There was one vase of chrysanthemums. The seats were the hardest kind of wood. There was a bubbly gas heater warming the vicar, and bats in the roof. Melinda knew vampires on sight. Mum knew why ladies wore hats in English churches.

No one knew the words; but there was worse to come. Dad sang the hymns, and singing had always been a strong point but not a good one. The organ bellowed and fought back. 'I won,' said Dad later. 'That harmonium hadn't an earthly.'

While the service went on, other things were happening. Not many people came, and the Skibathy family was the largest. Dad said the pew was like a loose box, and what was wrong with chairs? They weren't horses, after all.

To one side, at the front, there was a pew with a top to it, and an open front.

With a bit of glass in, it would have made a boutique.

'And look at that high-sided one,' Dad said. 'What do they keep in that and it won't show its face?'

Nobody sat in it. But something was going on there.

'Opossums in the roof,' said Dad. 'I can hear 'em.' But this was not an opossum: after a time it lit a pipe and smoke drifted across the church.

Mum wrinkled her nose. Dora held hers. 'If you've been shearing sheep all morning you can do with a puff,' said Dad, 'even if it's wattle leaves or rope-end, like this.'

'Hush,' said Mum. And the vicar looked at Dad.

'Just the gent in the horse box, mate,' said Dad. And everyone looked at him. 'Having a smoke.'

The vicar stepped to the door of the enclosed pew, opened it, and looked in. 'The squire's pew, and no one there,' he said. 'Now it is hymn 34.'

People looked round. Melinda felt ashamed of her family. Wayne saw something-or-somebody look out from the squire's pew and then not be there. It was a face or a cloud of pipe smoke. A face was bad enough, but pipe smoke meant a whole smoker. And there was no one there.

'Sing up,' said Dad, bumping him on the back. 'Hymn 34.'

That was the end of the service. The vicar stood at the door to see everyone out.

'That was very nice and tasteful,' said Dad, shaking hands. 'They last got me in one of those when I was married, and before that the padre would come round the shearing sheds beyond the black stump. We were all his sheep, he would say. We liked that.'

'I'm curious,' said the vicar. 'What brings you from beyond the black stump to the back of beyond here? The weekly bus?'

'In a way,' said Dad. 'My name is Skibathy, so when we saw the name on the bus I couldn't keep out. When I got here all the folk are called Wainwright, and that's my name too. So I reckon this

isn't the back of beyond to me.'

'We didn't know about it,' said Mum, 'until the train broke down in the station yesterday and we had to disembark. You don't know my husband. He follows everything up at once.'

'I know that about him,' said the vicar. 'He does.'

'And what's the secret about the smoke?' Mum went on.

'That's very odd,' said the vicar. 'Do you mean you had never heard of

Skibathy before yesterday?'

'They send all the bills to a family of that name,' said Dad. 'And before me there was my Dad. He always said we came from a long way back, but he never said where. Somebody from here settled in Australia, I reckon.'

'Might find it was a convict,' said Mum. 'That means a long time ago, ancient family, and that's good.'

The vicar went back into the building. 'People were sent out for nothing in those days,' he said. 'Come in and see whether the stones tell you anything. We'll look at the squire's pew.'

He led them there and opened the door. Dora climbed in and sat on a dusty cushion. She thought it was the queen's throne.

'Old Lord Granger sat here,' said the vicar. 'But not for a hundred years. They were all Wainwrights too, but the family died out. He used to light his pipe, just as he did at home. People say the smoke has been seen.' His voice echoed round the church, and his eyes shone a little larger.

'That's right,' said Dad. 'We all did.'

'But I don't think the squire was here,' said the vicar, firmly. 'Look along there.'

'There's a sort of carved hole,' said Dad. It was a notch in the oak, where something could be put in at the top but not pulled out at the front. Wayne put his fist in and proved it. 'What is it? A galah's nest?'

'Nearly,' said the vicar. 'Lord Granger put his watch there. It was a gold one, as big as a goose egg – called the golden egg. When the sermon was too long he rattled the lid. If it was too short he did the same. If he ran out of tobacco he went home. The curates were terrified of him, and the watch was called "The Egg-Timer".'

'I'll get a watch like that,' said Dad, 'for domestic use.'

'It was stolen,' said the vicar. 'Two hundred years ago.'

'It wouldn't have lasted this long,' said Dad. 'Well, it was strange about the smoke, but we've got to get back to our tucker without solving that mystery.'

'If I find anything more I'll let you know,' said the vicar. 'And I have to get back to my other parish.'

There was handshaking, and the rattle of doors being locked. 'There isn't a golden egg to steal,' said the vicar, 'but there's mischief to be done. Wait a minute, where's your other boy? Have we locked him in?'

'We've just got the one,' said Mum. 'Wayne, is that you?'

'I reckon,' said Wayne, and Melinda said, 'Swap any time.'

'You're . . . ? Well of course you're sure,' said the vicar. 'My mistake.' He went down to his car, gave a little bent wave, and drove away.

'He's worried,' said Dad.

Mum counted them. 'All here,' she said.

'Except Toota,' said Dora. She missed Toota.

Chapter 4

IN THE AFTERNOON, Dad stayed by the television and watched the beginning of the Rugby season. Mum unflew some of the journey by sleeping off jetlag. Melinda played Wayne at all the games in the pub, even the ones with cards or men lost from the pack. Mrs Wainwright came in at last to clear the table for afternoon tea.

'There's one missing,' she said. 'I'm right this time?'

'Dora,' said Melinda. 'Have you

seen her?'

'She's outside playing with your other boy in the rain,' said Mrs Wainwright. 'I don't know how you do it, but you've got two boys, and I see both and can't tell one from the other.'

'There's Wayne and his Dad,' said Melinda. 'Mum says they're both children.'

'I suppose disrespectful passes for polite in your country,' said Mrs Wainwright. 'But two boys you have, whether you know it or not.'

'What a line-out,' shouted Dad to the television. 'Get a heeler to nip their ankles.'

'And whatever language you speak,' said Mrs Wainwright, to the spluttering kettle in her kitchen.

Dora was playing a busy game on the lawn, jumping along a flagged path, giving orders with apparently no one there.

But there was. The other boy was standing in the shadow of a hedge, like a shadow himself. Wayne looked, and he wasn't. Then he unlooked, and the boy was.

'It's another you,' said Melinda. 'Yuk.'

Dora went on giving orders. Her hair was dark and clinging with rain, but she had not noticed.

The boy, in the same rain, was not wet at all.

'His hair's longer than yours,' said Melinda. 'And that's saying something.' She went too close, and the boy became invisible, as if he had been rubbed out. Melinda stepped back and the image reappeared. 'Power,' she said, doing it again. 'Who are you? Where are you from?'

The boy seemed to speak, but made no sound. His mouth moving might have been raindrops falling against the hedge.

'Stop interucting,' Dora shouted. 'He's called Wainwright and he's 'Stralian like us.'

No one understood that. Mum came out to bring them in. She had slept nicely and begun to feel she had arrived in England – not, she said, that any part of England was real. She began to think it was less and less real as the day went on.

First, she clearly saw the other boy, and spoke to him, thinking he was Wayne. 'Bring Dora in,' she said. 'She's wet through.' Dora was right across the lawn then, and could not have heard. The boy in the hedge spoke silently.

'Bring tea here,' said Dora, happy outside. 'Hello, Mum.'

'Now listen up,' said Mum, 'when I . . .'

'It's quite logical,' said Melinda,

because Mum was inclined to get angry when she did not understand the world. 'This one here is grotty old Wayne, that's Dora, I'm lovely me, and this one,' pointing to the other boy, 'is Wainwright and he's actually a ghost.'

'He wants to come back,' said Dora. 'I wish he would. He's better than Toota but he can't cuddle. I'm the only one what can hear him. I expect I'm magic.'

'Well, right on, a ghost,' said Dad, when Dora brought the boy in. 'I've just been watching pictures on the TV and they weren't real. You want an antenna and a set, and there the pictures are. So it's a ghost. I remember when there wasn't any television in Australia and when it came it was like magic until you saw the transmissions.'

'Magic,' said Dora. 'Sit next to me,' she told the ghost.

Dad was totally embarrassing, Melinda thought, passing cups and plates to a ghost. She told the boy to take no notice, but he wasn't anyway. Ghosts don't understand hot buttered crumpets no matter what poems say about eating toast.

Also she hated the way that the boy faded to nothing when anyone but Dora came near him. She told Dad about it.

'He's just shy,' said Dad. 'But stop putting your oar in. I'm trying to talk to

Dora about him.'

But Dora was busy with chocolate cake and her own dreams, and then wanted to sit on Mum. When she forgot the boy he went away entirely. Mum took Dora off to bed entirely too, and Mrs Wainwright took the remains of tea away. 'Except for the jam round Wayne's mouth,' said Melinda.

'So what do we know?' said Dad. 'He's from Australia and he's part of the family. Not many Australians can say that, eh? What did she mean, he turned the tram off and he turned the tick-tock on?' Dora had been explaining things.

'Tick-tock, he got us to the airport early, not to miss our flight,' said Wayne. 'That makes a lot of sense.'

'And the train broke down,' said Melinda. 'Right in the station. That's what she means.'

'He took me out of the station and I saw our name on the bus,' said Wayne. 'He did it all. He worked it.'

'I don't like being pushed around, I can tell you,' said Dad. 'I've been manipulated. But I want to know, so I'll bear with it.'

They found they did not know anything else. The ghost had brought them here and that was strange enough, a long way beyond chance. Dad brooded about it. 'I don't believe in ghosts,' he said. 'Never have. So where does that leave him?'

'It leaves you sticky-beaking into his affairs,' said Melinda.

'Yeah, yeah, yeah,' said Dad. 'But there's got to be more, there's got to be.'

Very soon there was more. Mrs Wainwright showed in another visitor, with water dripping from his hat.

It was the vicar. 'I'm so glad you haven't left yet,' he said, carefully counting Wayne to see there was only one of him.

'Good day, Padre,' said Dad. 'Have you come for the amber nectar, or just parish visiting?'

'I couldn't get our meeting this morning out of my mind,' said the vicar. 'Between services I looked in the old parish papers kept in the vestries. Americans and Australians often ask about their ancestors.'

'Ancestors don't run in our family,' said Dad. 'My Dad was just an orphan in Queensland. He didn't know where he was raised or who went before him.'

'But something came down the family,' said the vicar. 'I saw it. It brought you here. It wants you to know something, starting with the squire's pew.'

'It makes sense,' said Melinda. 'Come to think of it.'

'Sorry she's so uppity,' said Dad. 'She thinks men are idiots, I can tell you.'

'Very patronising,' said the vicar, being quite glad there was only ever one of Melinda. 'I looked back among the Wainwrights and found something very interesting, which no one has bothered about before. I copied it out.' He spread out some papers. 'This is the baptism certificate of John Wainwright, born

October 9, 1775. Jno is short for John,' he told Melinda quickly because she was getting picky about it. 'But on the back of it is the centre to the mystery. The vicar of that time wrote this on it: "May 13, 1787. This day the mute Jno Wainwright departs for Botany Bay guilty of theft last August".'

'Botany Bay,' said Dad. 'That's the first lot of convicts. He must have been some bad fellow.'

The clock in the hall outside chimed loudly thirteen times.

'What's mute?' asked Wayne.

'A reptile,' said Melinda.

'Deaf and dumb,' said the vicar. 'It wouldn't have helped.'

Wayne did mental arithmetic. 'He was eleven when he did the theft,' he said. Melinda counted on her fingers. 'And twelve years old when he went,' she said.

They had been doing different sums different ways. 'Thirteen when he got there,' said Dad, struggling with both kinds of sums and answers.

'Lucky not to have been hanged,' said the vicar. 'He was a very naughty boy, in spite of his handicap.'

At that moment there was a huge noise from outside, with glass breaking, metal smashing, wood splitting, and a ringing noise. Mrs Wainwright shrieked.

Chapter 5

DAD AND THE vicar opened the door
together. On the stone floor of the hall
there was a broken thing, split and burst,
with fragments all round it, a smashed
box.

'It's a coffin,' said Dad. 'My oath!'

'It's the roof fallen in,' said the vicar.

'It's my grandfather clock,' screamed
Mrs Wainwright. 'How did it happen?
Who did it? Someone could have been
killed.' She waved a large wooden spoon.

'We were all in the room,' said Dad,

taking the spoon away.

Mum looked down from the top of the stairs. 'Hush,' she said. 'She's just getting to sleep. Wayne, please.'

'The wood at the base has crumbled away over the years,' said the vicar, kneeling beside the remains of the clock. 'It's quite destroyed. Dead, you might say. It fell flat on its face. I'm afraid I don't know a suitable prayer, but it should have happened at midnight: they say a clock's praying then.'

He and Dad tidied the pieces away. Wayne picked up parts that had spread along the passage. Melinda swept up with a broom. 'Broken into minutes and seconds,' she said.

'Here's half an hour,' said Wayne. 'Where's the rest?'

'He did it,' said Melinda. 'Just when we said he was a naughty boy. But he can't

talk, and perhaps he isn't naughty.
Perhaps he's just trying to tell us.'

Mum came down. Mrs Wainwright,
upset and flustered, laid another place for
the vicar, and they had an evening meal.
Afterwards the vicar went on with what
he had found out.

'When Jno went to Botany Bay they probably labelled him Wainwright, because that was his name, and Skibathy because that was where he came from. If that's the case, then he was your ancestor, Mr Skibathy.'

'Call me Wainwright,' said Dad. 'If it isn't too confusing. That would go with what I know, but I don't know much.'

'We know more,' said the vicar. 'We know what was stolen.' Just as he said the words Dad jumped up, slapped his own wrist, then tore his watch off and dropped it on the table.

'It's red hot,' he said. 'Something wrong with the battery. That's the last time I have one of those.'

'The more things happen, the more I'm sure,' said the vicar, picking up the watch and burning his fingers, 'that this all hangs together. I don't think John

Wainwright stole what was stolen, and he's doing his best to tell us. The clock, your watch.'

'Thirty-third of August,' said Melinda.

'Sure,' said Dad. 'What was it? Anything interesting?'

Melinda was looking at Wayne, Wayne was looking at the vicar, the vicar was looking at Mum, and Mum was looking at Dad, who was looking at Melinda.

'Of course,' they said. 'That's it.' They had all understood what was going on, but no one was quite ready to explain it to the rest. What had been stolen was suddenly obvious. Other things were not.

Mrs Wainwright looked round the door before anyone spoke. 'Is it boiled eggs for breakfast again?' she asked. Which was very strange.

'Right on,' said Dad. 'Goose eggs, if you can.'

'Now I must go,' said the vicar. 'It has quite made my day. We can prove nothing, but we all understand the truth.'

No one had told Dora. She woke very early the next morning. Melinda found a cold draught creeping into her bed because the door was open. She got up to close the door and saw Dora in her nightie out in the road with Wayne, hand in hand. A second later she saw Wayne asleep in his room. Dora was going for a walk with the ghost, which might suit Dora but was not something elder sisters let happen. It was worse to steal Dora than to steal anything two hundred years ago.

She woke Wayne, and they both went out into the cold morning. The sky was blue and pink, and the grass at the road-side was white with drops of rain or dew.

'I thought he would have left,' said Wayne. 'Now we've sorted him out.'

'Then we haven't sorted him out,' said Melinda. 'They came this way.'

It was clear where Dora had gone. Her feet had scattered drops from the grass across a big field, leaving a shadow.

'His feet don't leave a mark,' said Wayne.

'Look, is that him?' said Melinda. But it was only a cloud of floating seeds from the dandelion clocks.

The track led through a stile with Dora's fingermarks on the top bar, across another field, and through a gateway into a grassy lane, with the shadow of little feet up its middle. Round a corner, they saw Dora walking with her friend the ghost boy.

'Jno Wainwright,' said Melinda.

'Do you think we should rescue her?' said Wayne.

'I don't know,' said Melinda. 'If it was him pushed the clock over, he might do something awful.'

'I'll strike midnight on him if he does,' said Wayne.

Away behind them they heard Dad helping Mum over a stile. She could manage very well on her own, but he wanted her to use his system, so there was a lot of noise.

'I'll go on after Dora,' said Wayne. 'You tell those two to stop their racket, or we shan't see what the boy does.' Melinda could make Dad obey, but he would argue with Wayne.

Dora led them up a hill between high banks, and to the edge of a clump of trees, a little spinney.

'We should see him off,' said Dad. 'That vicar could get rid of a ghost, with holy water and stuff.'

'He's your great-great-grandad,' said Melinda. 'He's more than two hundred years old.'

'I suppose he turned into a ghost of the age he was when this thing happened,' said Dad. 'If he hadn't done it, boy, would he be in despair! And imagine arriving in Sydney in those days, no McDonald's, no Safeway, no Opera House, nothing. I'll give him a bit more time.'

Dora went in among the trees. The rest of the family hurried closer. 'She's playing a game,' said Mum. 'She'll think she's lost in a minute, and there'll be gunfire. I'll go and get her.'

Chapter 6

BUT DORA HAD finished her journey.
Among the trees there was a little stone
building. It was falling to pieces, and one
of the trees had grown up through the
roof. A ray of early sunshine shone into
its doorway.

Dora looked round contentedly. She
had pleased the boy, and he had pleased
her. She gave Mum a beaming smile.

'Are you all right, darl?' said Mum.

''Course,' said Dora. 'This is a house.'
She went in.

'Watch that roof,' said Dad, hurrying forward anxiously.

'Don't upset her,' said Mum, holding his elbow.

Dora knew exactly what she was doing. At the empty doorway she lifted the latch and pulled the vanished door open and went in. She crossed the floor and tried to climb a ladder that was not there.

'Can't reach,' she said. 'The stable boy put it here.'

'I'll lift you up,' said Melinda. She was the best one at not disturbing her. 'Is this high enough?'

'Bit higher,' said Dora. 'What do I do now?' She was talking to the boy. 'Pull out the stone,' she told Melinda.

Melinda pulled. The stone did not want to come. Wayne went to help. He put the stone on the ground.

'Lift up again,' said Dora. When she was up she put her hand into the hole, then her arm, and felt for something.

'Finded it,' she said, and brought it out.

The sunshine flashed on it. Dad reached into his pocket where he now kept his watch. 'It's right,' he said. 'Dead to the minute. Just a couple of hundred years slow, that's all.'

Dora held it in two hands. It was the golden egg, big as a goose's, with a round face showing to one side, a tall loop at the top, a short gold chain, and a little winding key.

It had lain in the wall of this building since August 1786, waiting to show the right time at this moment, to be recovered because that time was right, because the Skibathy family was here, because the ghost of John Wainwright was here.

'Some chook laid that,' said Dad. 'Even

if it was a goose.'

'He saw the boy put it here,' said Dora.
'Then got sent to 'Stralia and couldn't
come to wind it. He talked to me.'

'We understand,' said Mum.
'Everything's all right.'

'He didn't steal it,' said Dora. 'But they
said he did. He didn't get no breakfast, and
they whipped him.'

There was a movement in the sunshine
at the doorway. There stood the boy, or
ghost, clear and distinct as reality, and
smiling to them all. He was plainly
happy. He turned his back on them and
walked off the way he had come. As he
went out of the sunlight he faded, until
there was nothing of him at all.

In Dad's hand, where the golden egg
lay, there was a sudden throb. The watch
came to life for a few seconds, chimed
eight o'clock, and then fell asleep again.

Later, in the church, it fitted its place in the squire's pew. And in London, with everybody including Toota watching, the Queen's jeweller opened it. Inside, it said 'George Wainwright, Baron Granger, 1726,' which was when it was made and who it was made for. And then the address, 'Skibathy,' which was who got it in the end. Now it is ticking away in Ivanhoe, Australia. It times eggs to a treat, and there are few sermons, even from Melinda.